WRATH OF D

A Dungeons and Dragons Adventure

D&D
MS

Dungeons & Dragons Made Simple

By

Nathan Keighley

CONTENTS

Introduction

About this book

This book includes a simplified iteration of the Dungeons and Dragons rule system, explained in a simplified way for new players to follow easily and start playing the game straight away. This book includes a rules summary, hints for players and adventures all together in one volume.

General introduction

One day, I read a comment online that stated: *"I've never really thought that D&D can be found in any book. You can start with them, sure, and you can use rules from books if they work for you, but to me, D&D has never been between the covers of a book. Making it your own and changing it and adding to it so that it works the way you want is the essence of D&D. Words on paper are not the game, the game is what we play."*

I couldn't agree more. For me, D&D is about the adventure, the make-believe, storytelling and escapism that comes with the game. The rules can be simply regarded as guidelines to facilitate the adventure, rather than strict laws to be adhered to. Indeed, the game creators have always asserted that Dungeon Masters should incorporate their own ideas and systems. *"Rules are nothing without the spark of life you give them"*.

I believe, and get the impression from reading comment sections, that many more people would be interested in playing the game, due to its appealing concept, but are put-off by the complicated rules or, at least, find it hard to encourage others to play with them on account of the effort involved in players familiarising themselves with the rules.

Therefore, I have gone through the 5th edition rules, which are free to download online, and attempted to summarise them to the bear minimum needed to play the game. Simple rules help to make game play flow, as less time is spent cross-referencing rules. It also helps get people involved who don't want all the rules, who want to play small episodes rather than great campaigns. Here character progression is less important and allows game play to be more spontaneous.

The Dungeons & Dragons roleplaying game is about storytelling, driven by imagination. The stories are structured, so that the adventurers' actions have consequences, and these might be determined by the roll of dice.

The game is narrated by the Dungeon Master (DM), who is the referee of the game and controls the monsters and events that happen in the adventure. The game starts with the DM reading a caption to describe the scene and this should be detailed and give hints to the objectives and challenges in the room.

Having listened to the room description, the players will perform an action to explore the dungeon. Often this might have consequences that the players will have to react to. Consider the example given here:

Read aloud: *"You enter a room containing four chests that are covered in dust, indicating that they have not been opened for some time. What do you do?"*

Options: investigate the chests. Some are trapped, players should search for and disarm traps. The DM will narrate the results of the adventurers' actions. *"You greedily open the chests in search of treasure and release a trap and receive d6 damage."* Conversely, the players will utilise a search action to look for traps, then roll a d20 to establish whether they can disarm them. *"You examine the chests and discover that they are trapped. You use your skill to disarm the traps before opening the chest to discover their contents."*

The game uses polyhedral dice with different numbers of sides. The different dice are referred to by the letter d followed by the number of sides: d4, d6, d8, d10, d12, and d20. The twenty-sided d20 is used most often for resolving actions made by the adventurers. For example, does the strike of a sword damage a monster, does an ogre believe your outrageous bluff or can the player swim safely to the other side of a river.

The success of actions depends on the capabilities of the characters. The capabilities are defined by six ability scores. The abilities are Strength, Dexterity, Constitution, Intelligence, Wisdom, and Charisma. These ability checks are made with the d20 and may also include **ability modifiers** added to the score. This roll will then be compared to a target number to determine the success of the action. If the total equals or exceeds the target number, the ability check, attack roll, or saving throw is a success. Otherwise, it's a failure. The target number is often referred to as a Difficulty Class (DC), or a monster's Armour Class (AC) during attacks. Each adventurer character is likely to have particular strengths and weaknesses. Their capabilities should be considered during gameplay. In the 5th edition rules you can learn how to create a character for Dungeons and Dragons. However, for the purpose of simplicity and timesaving, you can readily find pre-generated characters online. See also the chapter in this booklet that discusses choosing a character.

How to play

Introduction

The adventures that I write are designed in accordance with our *Dungeons & Dragons made simple* rules summary. This is for the purpose of creating accessible game formats in mind of new players, new dungeon masters, or people who simply wish to play a short game.

It is hoped that this simplification to the rules will help new players immerse themselves in the world of D&D and help to get their friends and family involved too. Enthusiastic players sometimes struggle to find a group, on account of the complexity of the game, so I created D&D Made Simple and the corresponding adventures with the intention of making a format of D&D that anyone can play and thereby help encourage new players into the game.

Game Overview

Step 1: choose a character – you can select from a range of characters, including humans, dwarves, elves and many more. Refer to appendix 2 to find pre-generated characters for this game.

Step 2: movement – your character sheet indicates how far you move (where 1 inch = 5 foot scale i.e., a character that moves 30 feet in a turn, moves across six inch-squares).

Step 3: describe the setting – the Dungeon Master (DM) will now read out a passage to describe the setting that the players have moved into.

Step 4: respond to encounter – the players will now make an action in response to the description of the setting for example 'search for traps' or 'listen at the door.' Actions might also require players to test their ability by rolling a twenty-sided dice (D20) and comparing their score to a target number. E.g., the door is jammed, roll a strength STR test [12] to open it.

Step 5: results of player actions – the DM will tell the players what the outcome of their actions is. E.g., they open the door, but set off a trap causing 1 hit point (HP) damage.

How to set up the game

You will need a grid of 1-inch squares, for example 5x8 inch grid (approx. A5) to represent the dungeon rooms. If you use a laminated sheet, or erasable board, you can draw on the features of each room that the players will interact with using a marker pen to save on printing sheets. The aim is to make a map that resembles the encounter.

For the adventurers and monsters, you can use miniatures, models, or make tokens to represent these characters when showing their positions in the rooms.

Use the map of the beast's labyrinth to track the positions of the players in the dungeon. Keep notes of the items that players have collected and their current HP status on printed character sheets (see appendix 2).

How to do combat

Simple combat encounters are performed by rolling the d20 and trying to beat the opponents armour class AC score for a successful hit, causing -1 HP damage. It is now the next players turn to make a combat roll. See appendix 1 for more details.

Equipment

A grid to map out the dungeon encounter, which can be a simple grid, or you can print tiles from the internet, with a simple dungeon tile image search, on A4 paper. Some people like modular tile systems, where smaller grid sections e.g., 3x3 inches are placed next to one another in various configurations. Another popular choice is the use of a battle mat with erasable markers to draw out the features of the game. You can also craft various terrain/furniture/landscapes to augment your game.

A twenty-sided dice (d20) is used to determine the success of most actions. A set of polyhedral dice are normally used to determine damage of attacks. Alternatively, you can just subtract average HP (hit point) per hit based on the character sheet e.g., d8 hit = -4 HP, or even play 1-hit deaths in high-risk adventure campaigns. It is nice to have a set of miniatures for the game, especially for the character players. However, the game can be played with tokens to represent people, creatures and objects. You can also print miniatures artwork images from online. I normally use a limited repertoire of monsters anyway. My favourite monsters include ogres, trolls, minotaur and dragons.

How to DM – the Dungeon Master, DM, is the referee of the game. The DM reads out the encounter description. The details of the encounter description set the scene and may contain important clues about the aspects of the environment that need to be explored, or hazards that should be avoided. The players will then take their first turn in exploring the dungeon. This might involve actions such as search, listen at doors, wisdom checks etc. The actions will have results, which are shown in the encounter bullet point notes and the DM responds to the players actions by reading out the results of their actions. This may need some improvisation, sometimes.

To determine the difficulty of a challenge, a target number [n] is given in brackets. This is what players must beat with a d20 roll. The challenge will relate to a specific ability check depending on the nature of the challenge e.g., strength STR for knocking down a door, or wisdom WIZ to understand the meaning of some symbols. It will be indicated in the encounter notes where ability checks are needed.

The dungeon layout will be shown on a schematic map. This is the guide for transferring the layout to a grid or tiles format in the table, such as printed A4 tiles (8x11grid). Always refer to the schematic layouts of dungeons. Sometimes adventures take place outside. These encounters might be represented by a schematic, or they may simply be described in words and the table layout of the encounter will depend on your interpretation of the environment description.

A location map is provided at the start of an adventure to give a reference to the setting by positioning the features of the adventure setting. Normally, encounters are played out on smaller arenas representing one locale of the entire location map.

Here I've set out simplified rules. **Ability scores** determine the capabilities of a player character. Modifiers are added to account for a character's proficiency in the ability. A challenge may present itself in the dungeon for which the DM decides which **ability check** is required to overcome the target number/difficulty class of the challenge.

So, the players encounter a challenge that requires an ability check, relating to one of the abilities listed below. They roll a d20, then add any modifiers noted on their character sheet and this gives their score. This score must be equal to, or greater than the target number [n] of the challenge.

- **Strength**, measuring physical power and athletics.

- **Dexterity**, measuring agility and skills such as Acrobatics Sleight of Hand and Stealth

- **Constitution**, measuring endurance and ability to withstand harms.

- **Intelligence**, measuring reasoning and memory, such as historical knowledge, power of investigation and knowledge of nature.

- **Wisdom**, measuring perception and insight including skills such as Animal Handling, Insight, Medicine, Perception, Survival, or finding a hidden object by using perception.

- **Charisma**, measuring force of personality, skills such as Deception, Intimidation, Coercion and Persuasion.

- **Speed of movement** is on the character sheet. Scale, 1 inch represents 5 feet.

- On your turn, you can move your speed then perform one action, or move your speed twice.

- Movement over rough terrain, you should half your speed.
- Task Difficulty, DC: Very easy 5, Easy 10, Medium 15, Hard 20, Very hard 25, Nearly impossible 30.

An ability check is made by rolling the d20, adding any modifiers to the score as necessary, and then determining how your score compares to the target DC. Here are some examples of using ability checks. Strength rolls are made to climb, swim, force open locked doors, break bonds etc. Dexterity is required to hide, disarm traps, pick a lock, securely tie a prisoner, wriggle free of bonds. A dexterity check is needed to determine **initiative** i.e., the order of whose turn it is in combat. For initiative, each player and monster roll a d20 dexterity check and the highest scorer goes first, and the lowest scorer last.

Engaging in combat: Strength roll for melee attacks and dexterity roll for ranged attacks. These rolls must equal or exceed the monster's armour class (given in the monster stat block). With a successful hit, take a damage roll (given on your character sheet as "hit dice" or as attack scores) and remove this number of hit points.

Healing wounds. I suggest using a medicine wisdom check to cure wounds with a DC of 15, then roll a d6 (or average 3) to determine how many hit points are recovered. I've added this rule to substitute the use of spells for healing, which are necessary to help preserve the adventurers after combat. Also, you can collect healing potions to restore d6 hit points.

For the use of magic, refer to the 5th edition rules. These are rather more complicated than the scope of this basic rules guide, so assume non-magical players with this rule system.

Experience points can be collected throughout an adventure to improve the capabilities of your character. However, they are omitted here because due diligence is needed to keep track of them and this can interfere with game flow, I find. Furthermore, this D&D system is designed in mind of occasional players that engage in the odd adventure, rather than full campaigns. In which case there is no point tracking XP. There are rules in the 5th edition for building encounters to match the XP level of characters. Review this if you want to progress with D&D.

Characters

In addition to the 5th edition rules of Dungeons and Dragons, you can also download a pdf of pre-generated characters for free. This saves time and complication. Go ahead and select a character that appeals to you.

The character sheet contains a lot of information about your character. However, it might be easier to navigate the information if the key attributes are summarised in a stat block, which clearly shows the essential information that is needed when performing actions and combat using this simplified D&D system described here.

This key information is summarised in the player character stat blocks that I have simplified from the official 5e pre-generated characters. Armour class is the target number for monster attacks. Hit points are how much damage you can take. These are the maximum value; you cannot gain more hit points than this. Subtract damage roll scores from your hit points. For example, a monster rolls a d20, successfully beating your armour class, then rolls a d8 and scores 4. You would subtract 4 from your hit points. Speed is given in feet, where 1 inch is 5 feet in the D&D 28 mm scale. Hit dice are the rolls that you make to determine damage against a monster. The following pages offer simplified pre-generated characters. Photocopy these sheets and hand them out to your players.

Human fighter

Armour class 17

Hit points 12

Speed 30 feet

Hit dice: 1d10

Strength STR (+3)

Dexterity DEX (-1)

Constitution CON (+2)

Intelligence INT (+0)

Wisdom WIZ (+1)

Charisma CHA (+2)

Items:

Dwarf cleric

Armour class 18

Hit points 11

Speed 25 feet

Hit dice: 1d8

Strength STR (+1)

Dexterity DEX (-1)

Constitution CON (+2)

Intelligence INT (+0)

Wisdom WIZ (+3)

Charisma CHA (+1)

Items:

Halfling rogue

Armour class 14

Hit points 9

Speed 25 feet

Hit dice: 1d8

Strength STR (-1)

Dexterity DEX (+3)

Constitution CON (+1)

Intelligence INT (+1)

Wisdom WIZ (+0)

Charisma CHA (+3)

Items:

Elf wizard

Armour class 12

Hit points 8

Speed 30 feet

Hit dice: 1d6

Strength STR (+0)

Dexterity DEX (+2)

Constitution CON (+2)

Intelligence INT (+3)

Wisdom WIZ (+1)

Charisma CHA (-1)

Items:

Human fighter

Armour class 14

Hit points 12

Speed 30 feet

Hit dice: 1d10

Strength STR (+2)

Dexterity DEX (+3)

Constitution CON (+2)

Intelligence INT (+0)

Wisdom WIZ (+1)

Charisma CHA (-1)

Items:

Adventuring

How to start building an adventure

Firstly, decide on a style of game play. Styles of game play might include the traditional dark dungeons with threat around each corner, few character interactions, numerous traps and hideous monsters to fight. By contrast, the DM can include more character social interactions, such as role-playing a tavern scene where information about the quest could be gleaned from the non-player characters. Outdoor settings can also be used, such as an adventure in the wilderness. Different methods can be used to build an adventure. Take the list of options below as a guidance:

- Have a series of encounters, which are played out in numeric order.
- Use random generated encounters. Create some individual encounter scenarios, number them,

then by rolling dice you can randomly select what happens.

- Have plotted routes. Intricately design a map of a dungeon, with numbered rooms that the players can explore room-by-room. Perhaps some routes are taken, while others are not.

Encounters are set out as a series of challenges. There is a description of the setting followed by a list of possible actions that the players could take, which effect the course of the narrative.

Mapping out the adventure – there are different means by which an adventure can be plotted out on paper and then translated to the tabletop. These include the use of maps, modular tiles, and battle grids. Dungeons can be built from modular tiles and a scale map of the layout is drawn in a notebook, with the locations of monsters, treasures and scenery annotated on it. For larger outdoor adventures, a battle mat can be set out with terrain scenery, such as houses, trees etc. set up on it. A sketch map of the layout would suffice to illustrate to the DM where things are located. Personally, I use a generic 8x11 A4 dungeon tile. I write a description of the room and use this as guidance on where to position props for the players to interact with.

Difficulty level – note that some campaigns might be harder than others and your characters might not be ready to take on all the challenges straight away. However, characters can choose to back away from an encounter that they don't feel ready for. Selecting an appropriate difficulty needs to be considered.

How to address difficulty level – You can play out the earlier campaigns multiple times to collect enough treasure to move forward to more challenging missions. For example, feel free to return to the marketplace as many times as you like to purchase equipment upgrades. By doing this, players will be in a more advantageous position for completing more challenging encounters, having better equipment. Here is a list of DM methods that can be used to moderate encounter difficulty.

- Include weapons upgrades e.g., a better sword that adds +1 attack modifier, or even include special weapons that involve better hit dice to standard character weapons. E.g., replace a d8 character hit dice with 2d10.

- Include alternative routes through dungeons that are safer for the players. They can therefore navigate a way through using wits rather than brawn.

- Create alternative ways to kill hard monsters. E.g., level 1 players won't be able to kill a dragon in normal combat, but maybe they can set a trap for it?

Overcoming challenges – periodically, there will be challenges in the game that your player characters must overcome. Challenges can take different forms. They could be physical challenges, such as booting down a locked door, or mental challenges, such as figuring out how to disarm a trap. Often these challenges will require a skills test by rolling a d20 to determine success, such as a strength roll, or an intelligence roll. The difficulty of a challenge should be relative to the twenty-sided dice outcomes.

Collecting items – during the campaign, your characters can acquire weapons upgrades, purchase foodstuffs to restore health and collect spells to advance their magic. These are detailed in the encounter. You can also steal these artefacts from defeated enemies. As the campaign progresses, it is necessary to keep an accurate account of players items and health status on their character sheet.

In addition to weapons and armour, you will collect gold and treasure, which can be represented on the tabletop by a token or treasure chests. Treasure has a value based on the items that it can be exchanged for when buying equipment.

The value of treasure – It is commonplace, while exploring a dungeon to discover treasures. Treasure can be valuable in an adventure if it can be used to purchase weapons upgrades, provisions and accoutrements. Often treasures are hidden in chests and may include various items such as gold, weapons and spells. However, jeopardy can be introduced to the game by including traps on treasure chests. The use of random treasure tables or lists of treasures or outcomes determined by rolling the dice can be a useful DM method. Chests can also be a good way of introducing essential items for the encounter. For example, the chest contains a key for a locked door, or an important magical item, such as a cloak of invisibility to avoid been seen by a dragon.

Random encounters – write several separate encounters (for example on index cards) and pick one at random to determine what happens next in your adventure. To avoid repetition in the future, you will need a large repertoire of random encounters. Chosen encounters must also be based on the location i.e., is the adventure in a dungeon or out in the wilderness?

Random encounters will be less intricate by design than planned adventures, but they have the advantage for a DM of being able to quickly put together an adventure without agonising over a plot. Random encounters will be short scenarios with a few options for diversifying how it is played out. They will also be generic. They are written in a brief manner with a short list of possible actions that the players can take. This is a great method for new DMs and players to get familiarised with the principles of the game. You can also include random monster encounters in these scenarios, if you like. Use this format to design numerous quick-fire encounters and combine them into an adventure.

In addition to having random encounter index cards, you can also have random monsters. This is achieved by creating a numbered list of dungeon monsters and rolling the dice to select which one you encounter. For example, a list of 10 monsters, roll d10 to select. This method can also be used to select treasures from chests using dice rolls to pick from a list.

Dungeons and dragons without a DM? – one advantage of random encounters is that you could autopilot the DM's role in the game by leaving encounters down to chance. By using random encounters selected with a dice roll, you can effectively cut out the DM and either join in with the adventurers or even implement a 1 player mode. However, the backstory, world building and role-playing will be markedly reduced in this style of gameplay.

In this section, I put together some brief ideas that you can use as templates and add to while creating your own adventures. Writing brief encounter ideas such as this can be a great way to introduce new players to the game, but also as a means to start designing your own campaigns, where there is more storytelling and role-playing required. The next chapter will explain how these ideas can be amalgamated into a proper Dungeons and Dragons campaign.

Roleplaying

In this chapter, I will give a detailed encounter guide for the DM. This will teach you how to be a DM. In the subsequent chapters, the encounters, which make up the adventure, are described. To start with, a description of the environment is read out by the DM. This description will contain clues to the important aspects of the encounter that the players should listen to and explore. The action of exploring is likely to result in an effect. These are described in the encounter notes and are also narrated by the DM and will influence future actions by the players.

Describing the table set-up – The use of dungeon tiles, such as my A4 sheet system, is common in Dungeons & Dragons. These take the form of a grid, often decorated to look like stone flags, that represent the room that the encounter takes place in. Sometimes, encounters take place outside and people often like to build terrain sceneries for this.

Before you start the adventure, hand out a copy of the setting map to the players along with a copy of either the 5e character sheet or the abridged character sheets that I created in this booklet. This will give the players a sense of direction when embarking on the encounters. The encounters occur numerically.

Adventuring – A D&D adventure may include various locations besides dungeons. A tavern encounter can be useful in Dungeons and Dragons to role play NPC interactions and allow your players to gain insights. It can also be an opportunity to gain rest and recovery. Markets can be a useful encounter for procuring goods that are beneficial to a campaign. Dungeons are the meat of the game where most of the combat happens, and magical items can be found. In between adventuring in dungeons, however, campaigns may also involve wandering in the wilderness.

During your adventuring campaign, it is likely that you will encounter magic items. These are objects that allow the players to gain abilities that will help them through challenging adventures. These may include:

Magic items

1. Amulet of health – gives you a constitution score of 19.
2. Armour (light, medium and heavy) gives you an armour class bonus (+1, +2, +3).
3. Elven cloak, by pulling the hood up you gain +1 on wisdom and dexterity checks.
4. Gauntlets of ogre power – gives you a strength score of 19.
5. Healing potions.
6. Spell scrolls.
7. Ring of protection – gives you a +1 bonus to armour class.
8. Weapon (common, rare, very rare) gives you a bonus to attack and damage (+1, +2, +3).

Monsters

Here I have included a subset of common dungeon monsters in this prepared stat block. However, for a complete list, I would refer to the 5th edition rules. Furthermore, I have simplified the monster stat blocks for easier game play. Please refer to the 5th edition rules for a full description of actions.

Describing stat blocks – I've removed the ability scores because monsters are often involved in combat and less often in social interaction when compared to the players. This helps to simplify the stats, which include armour class **AC** (the target to beat with your strength roll in combat), hit points **HP** (the number of hits the monster can take), the speed and the hit score, that is used to take damage against your characters hit points.

Stat blocks

Monsters	AC	HP	Hit score	speed/ ft
Adult red dragon	19	256	19	40
Awakened tree	13	59	14	20
Constrictor snake	12	13	6	30
Gargoyle	15	52	5	30
Ghost	11	45	17	40
Giant rat	12	7	4	30
Giant spider	14	26	7	30
Goblin	15	7	5	30
Hill Giant	13	105	18	40
Minotaur	14	76	17	40
Ogre	11	59	13	40
Orc	13	15	9	30
Poisonous snake	13	2	5	30
Skeleton	13	13	5	30
Troll	15	84	11	30
Young dragon	18	136	15	40
Zombie	8	22	4	20

Swarms of creatures

Swarms	AC	HP	Hit score	speed/ft
Bats	12	22	5	30
Insects	12	22	10	20
Poisonous snakes	14	36	7	30
Rats	10	24	7	30

Map of setting

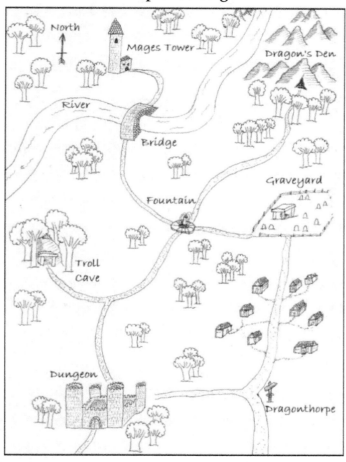

The Beast's Labyrinth

[Read aloud to the adventurers]

An Ogre has stolen the Duchess' prize stallion and demands a ransom of 500 gold. You and your fellow adventurers enter the beast's labyrinth in search of gold and jewels to pay the Ogre, knowing that a monster still guards the treasures within...

Dungeon master's notes

Start each encounter by reading out the setting description to the players. The players will now take their turn by performing an action. The bullet point notes beneath the encounter description list the possible actions that players can take that will help them to move forwards in the game. Some improvisation will be needed here to keep continuity in the game. When the players have responded to the challenges set out in the encounter, the list of options will indicate the consequences of those actions. Steps 1-5 have been completed, now repeat this process as the players move to the next challenge.

Don't play the encounters in numerical order. The numbered encounters are based on the room numbers, which will be played out based on the players movement through the dungeon. Each encounter will have multiple doors and therefore several route options are available to the players as they explore the beast's labyrinth. Therefore, it is important to keep track of whereabouts the players are in the dungeon as the game progresses.

Note that the objective of the game will be to collect 500 gold value of treasure, in accordance with the adventure description, to pay a ransom. Will your players survive this ordeal in the beast's labyrinth?

Map of the Beast's Labyrinth

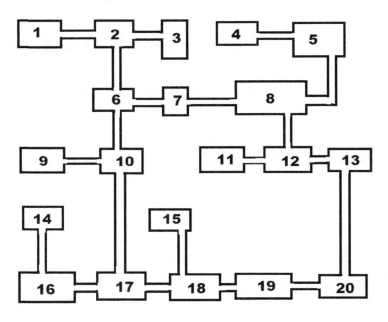

Encounter 1 – A Pile of Crap

[Read aloud] You enter the first room in the labyrinth and see a rather large dung pile discarded at the entrance to the dungeon. Maybe the monsters hiding in here have got plumbing problems? Anyway, the smell is unpleasant for anyone coming to the door. What do you want to do?

- Investigate the door – it is locked and requires a key (hidden in dung pile).
- Break into the labyrinth STR [16].
- Search in the dung pile – [Read aloud] while rummaging in the dung, you come across the key for the door. However, in the process you disturb a swarm of insects, and they attack. See monster stats.
- Use the key that was found in the dung to open the door into room 2.

Encounter 2 – The Serpent's Lair

[Read aloud] You enter the next room in the labyrinth and see a giant constrictor snake coiled around a chest. It awakens upon your entry but does not come to attack you and remains coiled around the chest. There is a door close behind where the snake is sitting and another door to the right, further from the snake. What do you want to do?

- Head towards the door to room 3 – the door is open, but the players aggravate the snake by coming closer and are withing striking distance.
- Players that have found a flute and have learnt the correct tune to play INT test [8] can tame the snake to sleep and enter room 3 unobstructed.
- Head towards the door on the right to room 6. The door is unlocked.
- Combat the snake – see appendix 4 for details.
- Search the chest – in contains 20 gold pieces and a key with the Greek letter lambda on the handle.

Encounter 3 – The Precarious Vase

[Read aloud] You enter the next room in the labyrinth and see and expensive-looking vase on a plinth, what do you want to do?

- Collect the vase (worth 100 gold) – triggers a trap causing (-3) HP.
- Search for traps – requires a WIZ test of [14] to find this trap, then a DEX test of [12] to disarm it to safely collect the vase. Otherwise, the trap is triggered.
- Leave and return to room 2.

Encounter 4 – Hostile Ornaments

[Read aloud] You enter the next chamber in the labyrinth and see three grotesque statues with wide open mouths in a line along the room. At the far end of the room, there is a chest. You are about to go across and investigate it, when a torrent of flames is fired from the mouth of one of the statues. What do you want to do?

- [DM note] the three statues shoot fire across the room in the order 2, 3, 1 when numbered along the room. Players can wait three turns to decipher this sequence and avoid the flames (-4 HP damage).
- Leave the room and return to room 5.
- Investigate the chest, which contains 40 gold pieces and a ruby worth 20 gold.

Encounter 5 – The Imperishable Flame

[Read aloud] You head around a corner in the corridor and come into the next room in the labyrinth and see an imperishable fire burning without fuel. Bookshelves surround the room and ahead there is a door leading to the next chamber. What do you want to do?

- Investigate the door – it is locked and cannot be opened with brute strength or even with a key. WIZ test [12] reveals that it is locked with a magic spell.
- Search the bookshelves – the books contain spells. Add the right spell to the fire to get through door. [Read aloud] You find three books of interest. They seem to contain spells. The titles of each are as follows: Book 1: *Sorcerers Guide to Necromancy*; Book 2: *Spellcasting Scrolls of Security*; Book 3: *Wizards Herbal Handbook*. [DM note] players must burn Book 2 to break the spell to unlock the door and enter room 4. If

the wrong books are burnt, the fire explodes, causing (-6) HP to all players.

Encounter 6 – In the Doghouse

[Read aloud] You enter the next room in the labyrinth and see a large dog standing over a trapdoor. What do you want to do?

- Fight the dog – appendix 4 for stats.
- Lift the trapdoor – Once the dog is dead [Read aloud] inside the chamber under the trapdoor is a chest containing an assortment of goods. There is a rare sword (+1 to attack scores). A length of rope, a broken harp, a healing potion

(restores all HP) and a flute bearing the emblem for a serpent upon it and a gold ring worth 10 gold pieces.

- Head through the door to room 10 – it is locked and has the Greek letter lambda inscribed upon it. The door requires the key with this symbol to be opened.
- Head through the door to room 7 – it is open.
- Return to room 2.

Encounter 7 – Ghastly Gargoyle

[Read aloud] You enter the next room in the labyrinth and see a gargoyle in the centre of the room. Water pours from its mouth into a basin at its feet. Upon the basin are written some demonic symbols that are hard to understand. What do you want to do?

- Drink from the water in the basin – the water is refreshing and restores +3 HP.
- Move past the gargoyle and head to the door leading to room 8 [Read aloud] As you pass by the gargoyle, the stone statue awakens then attacks you.

- Read the symbols – take an INT test [9] to decipher the meaning: [Read aloud] "only a ring bearer may pass the gargoyle else his quest ends in turmoil." [DM note] players need to find rings in the dungeon to pass into room 8, otherwise the gargoyle awakens and attacks.
- Return to room 6.

Encounter 8 – Singing Sirens

[Read aloud] You enter the next room in the labyrinth and see a beautiful siren singing a captivating song. You are enticed closer to her by her wonderful voice.

- Take a CON test [12] to avoid being enticed closer by the singing. The siren turns into a harpy and gets a surprise attack on captivated players.
- Players with a successful CON roll realise the siren is a monster and can attack first.
- Search the body of the harpy to find a key with the Greek letter Omega on the handle.
- Head to room 5 – the door is locked and has the Greek letter Omega inscribed upon it.
- Head to room 12 – the door is unlocked.
- Return to room 7.

Encounter 9 – Sewer Rats

[Read aloud] You head down a set or stairs and enter the next room in the labyrinth which appears to be a sewer. The atrocious smell of the sess pool discourages you from going further, but it could be worthwhile braving the gases to search for hidden gems.

- Go into the sewer – players are attacked by pack rats (see appendix 2, swarm of rats' stats).
- Search the sess pool in the middle of the sewer chamber – [Read aloud] the water is deep and mirky, who knows what could be lurking at the bottom (find a key with the Greek letter Gamma on the handle by swimming in the sess pool, CON test [10] needed to avoid -4 Hp damage, and three gems worth 100 gold altogether) and two gold rings worth 20 gold pieces.
- Return to room 10.

Encounter 10 – Spirit Guardian

[Read aloud] You enter the next room in the labyrinth. It appears to be an empty passage, but then a ghost manifests from the ether and says to you: "To pass this way, answer my question. The bull-headed man has hasty hooves and wanders this maze for the rest of his days. What is the monster of whom I speak?" What do you want to do?

- Attempt to run past the ghost and enter another room – the ghost follows the players and attacks them (see appendix 4 for fighting the ghost.
- Attempt to answer the ghost's questions and gain safe access through this room (answer: *Minotaur*).
- Decline to give and answer and return the way you came.

Encounter 11 – Locked Out

[Read aloud] You head towards the next room in the labyrinth and approach the door, which has a coded padlock on it. Whatever is behind this door must be valuable given that it is so well secured.

- Investigate the lock – the lock has four random numbers. These must be adjusted to the correct sequence in order to gain access to the room.
- Note the prisoner in encounter 15 has the code for the door, which reads 5, 8, 11, but the last number is smudged, and the players cannot make it out, so must figure out that $3n+2$ is the function for the code, therefore the last number is 14.
- Unlock the door and enter the room – inside the room, there is a pile of gold heaped in the centre. You estimate that there are 100 pieces in total.
- Return to room 12.

Encounter 12 – Many Harmful Heads

[Read aloud] You enter the next room in the labyrinth which is brightly lit by flaming torches around the room walls and in the middle of the chamber, you see a hideous hydra.

- Note: use stat for constrictor snake for reach of the three heads.
- Use the torches around the room – cut of its three heads and burn the stumps, otherwise the heads grow back (make sure to tell the players about the heads growing back).

Encounter 13 – The Bony Men

[Read aloud] You follow the injured hydra into the next room in the labyrinth and watch as it writhes in pain and finally dies. What do you want to do?

- Search the dead hydra – you find a key, with the Greek letter beta on the handle, tied to a string around one of the severed heads. [Read aloud if players grab the key] You reach for the key and the teeth drop out of the skull and serve as seeds to produce a room full of animated skeletons (six enemies) which you must fight.

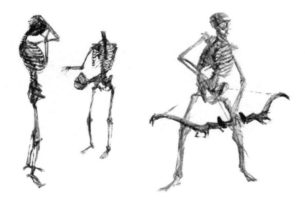

Encounter 14 – Shepards Shelter

[Read aloud] You enter the next room in the labyrinth and see a room full of sheep bleating, then suddenly the minotaur comes into the room. What do you want to do?

- Fight minotaur.
- Try to run (the minotaur follows players around the dungeon).
- Hide amongst the flock DEX test [8].

Encounter 15 – In Jail

[Read aloud] You enter the next room in the labyrinth and find a prisoner in shackles: he gives you a warning, "the gold isn't worth the risk my friends, leave me here and flee!" What do you want to do?

- Leave him here and move on, there's nothing can be done to help him.
- Try to convince the prisoner to help you find the gold. CHA test [8] needed to persuade him to give you a note.
- Try to break the prisoner's shackles and free him, STR test [14]. In gratitude, he gives you a note.
- The note – the prisoner has the code for the padlocked door, which reads 5, 8, 11, but the last number is smudged, and the players cannot make it out, so must figure out that $3n+2$ is the function for the code, therefore the last number is 14.

Encounter 16 – The Treasure Chamber, at Last

[Read aloud] You enter the next room in the labyrinth and see a room filled with chests overflowing with gold and jewels. What do you want to do?

- Start to collect the gold – [Read aloud] As you collect the gold, the shiny metal turns to sand in your hands and you realise that you have fallen victim for a spell of deception. Next, you hear a loud creaking noise, and a trapdoor opens up causing you to fall into a pit trap, and there you must remain until rescued.
- The other adventurers will have to use a length of rope collected from another encounter to come back and rescue the fallen player from the pit trap.
- Inspect the treasure with a WIZ test of [8] the players notice that the gold does not seem normal, something isn't right.

- Head to room 14 – the door is locked and has the symbol Gamma inscribed on it (needs matching key).

Encounter 17 – A Tight Squeeze

[Read aloud] You enter the next room in the labyrinth and almost immediately, the walls start to close in, sealing the room off. A poster on the far walls says how to stop them. It states: "Praise the master of this abode, and the movement of the walls shall hold." What do you want to do?

- To stop the walls closing in, the players must praise the minotaur in some way, e.g., *"Minotaur, you have the most handsome horns in the land."*
- Leave this room and find another route. Note that this will close room 17 off to the players for the rest of the game.

Encounter 18 – Bats Out of Hell

[Read aloud] You enter the next chamber in the labyrinth and see a flock of bats roosting, hung on the ceiling. What do you want to do?

- Players must mention that they move through stealthily, DEX test [15] to avoid disturbing the swarm of bats, leading to a battle encounter.
- Head to room 15 – the door is locked and has the symbol Beta inscribed ion it (needs matching key).

Encounter 19 – The Beasts Bedroom

[Read aloud] You enter the next room in the labyrinth and see that the minotaur is sleeping on a bed of hay. It is snoring loudly, but the snoring stops when you attempt to tiptoe past. What do you want to do?

- A DEX test [16] is needed to get past without making noise and awakening the beast.
- Get a surprise attack on the minotaur first while it sleeps, then engage in combat.
- Search the minotaur's body (requires DEX test [18] while sleeping), you find a pouch containing three jewels worth 100 in gold.

Encounter 20 – Don't Lose Your Head

[Read aloud] You enter the next room in the labyrinth and see a severed head but is speaks to you. "Watch out for the sleeping beast, you won't find the gold in here anyway. It's all locked up safe, apart from the crown jewels, that is, ha-ha. Lost my head trying to get those!" What do you want to do?

- Leave the severed head and move off to another room.
- Attempt to persuade the head to tell you where the treasure is kept CHA test [16] reveals, [Read aloud] the gold is kept locked in the treasure chamber, you will need the pass code to get in there. The crown jewels, though, are in the minotaur's belt pouch, good luck getting those.

Wandering the Wild Woods

About this adventure

The setting of this adventure is the Wild Woods. A dangerous, mystic fantasy woodland, with unforeseen perils at every corner. The adventure starts in the wild woods and leads to various other locations in the story setting. These locations include Evergreen Hamlet, the wizard's apothecary tower, the Wild Woods and Timber bridge. Each location includes a series of encounters for the adventurers to explore. They can return to a location to complete some encounters later. They don't need to sequentially finish all the encounters before moving on to another location. They are free to move around the setting. Set the tabletop up from your imagination, based on the descriptions of the encounter settings.

Encounter 1 – An Unpleasant Encounter

[Read aloud] You encounter the fabled ogre of Evergreen Hamlet and are drawn into combat. Do you continue to fight or flee?

- The ogre will appear from an edge of the board (number the edges and roll d4 to determine which edge) and move his speed. He will continue to walk along a straight path through the woods unless he spots the players with a WIZ test [16] and will attack.
- [DM note] fighting the ogre will be difficult for the adventurers, unless they have collected equipment to give them an advantage and return to this encounter later.
- Player actions can include combat, fleeing to the edge of the board to escape the ogre, or hide behind some terrain scenery DEX test [12].

Encounter 2 – A Short Cut to Mushrooms

[Read aloud] You stumble across a patch of mushrooms. They are pale-coloured and have a generally unassuming appearance.

- Eat them to restore some energy. They taste bland but you feel better for eating them +1 hit point. [or] They are poisonous, and you are sick. CON test [16] to avoid taking d4 damage. DM to choose.
- Collect them for later, or to sell at the village for 5 gold. Players can return to the mushroom patch in this encounter any time.

Encounter 3 – Scattered Leaves

[Read aloud] As you continue to walk through the woods, a gust of wind blows a chill breeze between the trees and scatters the fallen leaves from last year across the forest paths. You can no longer make out where the trails are and where the scrubland is. What do you want to do?

- Search the leaf litter.
- [Read aloud] You trigger a trap that was set to capture some unfortunate animal. DEX test [14] to avoid the trap and d8 damage.
- [Read aloud] You find a poisonous snake in the leaflitter. Its venom could be useful, or do you leave it be? (Engage in combat with poisonous snake to collect venom.)

Encounter 4 – A Sense of Direction

[Read aloud] After wandering aimlessly lost in the woods, you eventually reach a junction in the road and find an old signpost that offers some sense of direction. The signpost indicates that the SE Road leads onwards along Forest Lane towards Evergreen Hamlet. The NW Road leads towards the river crossing at Timber Bridge. Or you can continue your journey through the woods. Where would you like to go?

- Head down the SE road towards Evergreen Hamlet, move to Encounter 12.
- Head down the NW road towards the river crossing, move to Encounter 11.
- Continue through the woods, move to Encounter 5.

Encounter 5 – Strange Trees

[Read aloud] In this part of the forest, the trees look more characterful, some even appear to have faces. Ahead from the characterful trees are thick thorn bushes. Do you continue this way or head back to the signpost?

- Investigate the trees. [Read aloud] as you look at the tree, a voice calls out: "Riddle tree, riddle tree that is me. Answer my riddle and I'll leave you be. We grew from an acorn, did us three. What kind of tree are we?"
- Answer correctly (Oak tree) and nothing happens. Incorrect answer… [Read aloud] Suddenly one awakes and attacks you. Can you outrun a tree? Or make matchsticks of it.
- Leave this area and head onwards. [Read aloud] This part of the woods has thick thorn bushes under the canopies. You will have to work hard to hack your way through. Lose 1 HP.

Encounter 6 – The Cabin in the Woods

[Read aloud] A cabin in the woods is ahead of you. It looks old and dilapidated, but there is smoke coming from the chimney. Do you decide to take a look inside.?

- Roll d6 to determine what you find (1) chest containing 10 gold coins (2) poisonous snake (3) cauldron containing healing potion, enough to restore 1 HP to each adventurer (4) cauldron contains poison, d4 damage. (5) food cooking over a fire +1 HP if eaten. (6) the room is trapped DEX test [16] to avoid d4 damage.

Encounter 7 – Happy Campers?

[Read aloud] In the distance, you spot the glow of fire as you steadily approach a campsite. Do you want to investigate it?

- The campsite belongs to an ogre. He is currently asleep. DEX [15] stealth test to pass through undetected. Otherwise, the ogre is alerted and attacks.

[Read aloud] as you tiptoe through the campsite, you spot a large chest and a large cage with a cloth over it. Do you dare to investigate these objects, or do you continue to sneak through the campsite?

- [Read aloud] The chest is a lure, and you find yourself trapped in a net and with an ogre running out of the woods towards you. Make a STR test [14] to cut yourself free in time to run from the ogre; [10] you cut yourself free, but now you are faced with a hungry ogre to fight. Rolls less than [8] and you are dinner.
- Search around the campsite. [Read aloud] Close to the campsite, you find a large cage containing

three children. they plead to you not to hurt Elizabeth whoever that might be?

- Players can release the children from the cage and collect a reward of 10 gold when they arrive at Evergreen Hamlet.
- Players can attack the ogre in his sleep (surprise attack, roll hit dice without having to beat AC score) then engage in combat.
- Set traps in the campsite. DEX test [10] to successfully hide them, cause d10 (or 5) damage when triggered.

Encounter 8 – At the Riverbank

[Read aloud] You arrive at the river. What do you want to do next?

- Swim across STR test [12] and move on to the mage's tower/apothecary (Adventure Part 2).
- Walk N to find timber bridge (move to Encounter 11).
- Walk S, you are hopelessly lost and must return the way you came. Lose 1 HP.

Encounter 9 – Make for the Hills

[Read aloud] You reach a rocky outcrop in the forest and the trees are less tightly packed. Would you like to investigate this area, or move onwards?

* [Read aloud] As you are walking close to the cliff face, loose rock falls towards you. DEX [12] to avoid d8/taking 4 damage.

[Read aloud] It is rumoured that the troll living in a cave in the woods, down the west road, has numerous treasures stashed within his abode. You journey down the west road, through the woods and towards the hillside. There you find the cave entrance. An obnoxious odour emanates from the entrance. You creep silently inside. The troll is sleeping inside the cave. Around him, rubbish is strewn everywhere. Rotting animal carcases, pieces of firewood and bags of bones litter the floor. However, among this trash you espy the glint of sparkling treasures. Curiosity tempts you further inside.

- Search for treasure – players will need a dexterity roll DEX [12] to stealthily search for treasure. If you roll a score less than [12], the clammer of your searching wakes the troll and it attacks. Players can search as many times as they want, but don't wake the troll!
- Open treasure chests – the DM can decide what to contain within them, gold, weapons, armour etc.
- Attack the troll – make the first attack while the troll sleeps and a fight will ensue after the hit dice have been rolled. There's no need to make a strength combat roll first, it's a surprise attack.

Encounter 10 – Stuck in the Mud

[Read aloud] You arrive at a bog. The soft ground squelches under your footsteps which sink to knee depth in the mud, but the tussocks offer firmer ground. What do you do?

- Walk across the bog CON [16] to avoid losing a hit point through exhaustion.
- Search around in the bog WIZ [8] – you find a hidden chest that contains 20 gold pieces, an old rope, and a cloak of deception (+3 to DEX stealth rolls).
- Use the rope that can be used to pull one another through the terrain.
- Hop between the firm tussocks to cross easily.

Encounter 11 – Timber Bridge

[Read aloud] you wander along the road towards the river crossing at Timber Bridge. As you stroll down the path, you are met by a traveller. He is a merchant, who had to abandon his wares on the road. He is eager to sell food items to the local townsfolk but had to abandon the wagon at the other side of the river because the bridge was unsuitable to cross over. He explains his predicament to you. Do you want to help him?

- Return to the crossroads (encounter 4), you don't fancy tackling the bridge right now.
- Cross the river to investigate the wagon.

[Read aloud] You arrive at Timber Bridge. It is an old wooden bridge that is composed of heavily weathered boards. Many of the boards are missing and there is no way the merchant's wagon would get across. Clearly the bridge has had little use, the only tracks in the road are of the wagon tracks and some large footprints that follow the wagon tracks and then head off into the Wild Woods. The river is flowing fast after the recent rain. What do you want to do?

- Repair damaged bridge to enable a safe crossing. Repair by felling a tree for timber and use carpenters' tools from the merchant's wagon to craft new boards.

- Attempt to cross the bridge in its current state of disrepair. Players must only cross one at once, making a DEX test [12]. else it will break, and they fall into the river.
- Attempt to swim across the river STR test [16].
- Look for a slower/narrower point to cross by venturing into the woods (move to encounter 7, the campsite).
- Follow the footprints into the wild wood (move to encounter 7, the campsite).
- WIZ test [10] you realise the footprints belong to an ogre.

[Read aloud] You cross the bridge and continue down the road. Half a mile down, you see the abandoned wagon. What do you want to do next?

- Turn around and return to the old signpost (encounter 4).
- Investigate the cart.
- Does the ogre return? – 50/50 chance he will (flip a coin or roll dice, odd vs even, to see). The ogre has a surprise attack on the players if there is no

lookout. If there is a lookout, the ogre is seen approaching the wagon.

- Assign a lookout to check for the ogre – If the ogre returns, [Read aloud] the ogre is spotted in the distance returning to the wagon. Thanks to your lookout, you have time to flee or make ready to fight.
- Search the wagon for goods. See list of wagon contents. Adventurers can only take 1 item each but can return and swap items.

(1) healing potion
(2) fire starters
(3) carpenters' tools
(4) food items
(5) large traps x5

Encounter 12 – Evergreen Hamlet

[Read aloud] An ogre torments Evergreen Hamlet and kills anyone who tries to leave the village. Residents are on the brink of starvation, but not all is as it seems.

You stroll into the village. It is a small settlement with only around a dozen thatched cottages. You see a few of the locals wandering about, they look sullen, and no wonder given the stories of the ogre that has been terrorising the village. What do you want to do?

- Leave Evergreen Hamlet, for now.
- Speak to villagers (NPCS, Non-Player Characters), asking them any questions that you might have.

(1) is it true about the ogre? [Read aloud] *"aye, it is. He showed up around the same time as that wizard came to the tower. Ever since, anyone who leaves the village doesn't come back."*

(2) is there any food to be had? [Read aloud] *"not a mouthful. We'd be grateful to anyone who'd bring us*

something to eat right now. We're starving here. There was supposed to be a supply wagon on its way, but we've not heard a thing." (Adventurers can collect pumpkin soup from the wizard's garden, mushrooms from the woods, or collect food items from the abandoned wagon and deliver them to the village for a reward of 20 gold pieces).

[Read aloud] Each week, a child has gone missing from the village. Rumours point to the dreadful ogre. The village alderman offers to pay a handsome reward [bracelet of fortitude, +3 AC] if the missing children are returned.

- Start searching the village for clues. [Read aloud] As you stroll around the village investigating the case of the missing children, you notice a set of large footprints, much larger than those of a human, leading away from the village and into the Wild Woods. WIZ test [8] reveals that these are ogre footprints. Adventurers can follow the footprints back to the campsite in encounter 7.

- Talk with the alderman to learn clues about the missing children and the whereabouts of the ogre. [Read aloud] *"My daughter, Elizabeth was the first to go missing. She was out playing in the pumpkin patch in the apothecary gardens. I ventured into the woods to collect mushrooms, came back, and she was gone. After that, several other children have disappeared. All evidence leads to them being taken by the ogre, living in the woods."* [Read aloud] recognising you as great warriors, the alderman hires you to kill the ogre that has plagued the village. He has a particular interest in receiving the head of the ogre, as his daughter Elizabeth was the first child to go missing. What do you want to do?
- Head into the wild woods searching for the missing children (Encounter 7).
- Cross timber bridge to go to Adventure Part 2.

The Wizard's Apothecary

About the adventure

In this adventure, the players visit the wizards tower, where he sets them a series of missions to complete that revolve around his experiments with potions in the apothecary.

Encounter 1 – Voracious Vegetables

[Read aloud] The resident wizard, while experimenting with potions, has caused the pumpkins in the vegetable patch outside the apothecary to become sentient and carnivorous. The locals of Evergreen Hamlet want their squash problem squashed and offer 10 gold as a reward.

As you approach the wizard's garden, you read the notice that offers the amulet of protection, [+2 AC] to stop the rampant pumpkins. The pumpkins have prevented the wizard from leaving his apothecary tower. Meanwhile, the pumpkins come bouncing over towards you. What do you do?

- Combat the pumpkins. They deal 1 HP damage per successful d20 attack roll against the adventurer's armour class. Each pumpkin that is destroyed produces two more and the pumpkins can multiply infinitely.
- Alternatively, burn the garden patch, using fire starters collected from the abandoned cart. This will destroy the pumpkins.

- Flee the wizard's garden and return to Evergreen Hamlet.

Encounter 2 – The Magic Ingredient

[Read aloud] The wizard is thankful for your rescue from the pumpkins, and he offers you a job to do. The wizards' apothecary needs a special ingredient. The venom of a poisonous snake, gathered on a moonlit night. Where could this item be found, you wonder?

- Search in the wild woods for a snake. Replay the wild woods encounter until the adventurers find a poisonous snake.
- Decline the job for now and move to another location.

Encounter 3 – Re-stocking the Shelves

[Read aloud] You return with the poisonous snake venom in a glass vial. The wizard is away from the apothecary, apparently enjoying his freedom since the imprisonment from the pumpkin patch, so you enter the tower and place the vial on one of the shelves, labelled snake venom. There are many other shelves full of potion bottles, scriptures, books and jars of assorted animal parts. The wizard has obviously been very busy, as his workbench is cluttered with these items also. What do you want to do next?

- Leave the apothecary and return to the signposted crossroads, encounter 4 of adventure 1.
- Search the apothecary shelves. [Read aloud] Among the selection of potions you find two bottles of healing potion. Surely, the wizard wouldn't mind you taking them, after all you did help him.

- Search the potions workbench. [Read aloud] Among the clutter on the workbench, you glance over several scriptures that contain recipes for potions. You open a large, leather-bound book to the marked page, which discusses potions used to transform creatures into larger brutish beasts.

Encounter 4 – Rodent Rampage

[Read aloud] The apothecary has been dumping rejected potions into the river. Mutated giant rats now threaten to overrun the hamlet.

- Combat the (5) giant rats.
- Set traps, obtained from the abandoned wagon. DEX test [10] to successfully hide them, cause d10 (or 5) damage when triggered.

Journey to Dragon Thorpe

About the adventure

The adventurers have arrived and the main town in the campaign setting. This can be a useful place for them to regather their strength between adventures and to purchase weapons and armour upgrades to help with future missions. However, don't remain there too long, as the future isn't bright for Dragon Thorpe, as the town eventually becomes raided by monsters and hence forth is known as 'Old Town.'

Encounter 1 – A Drink in the Tavern

[Read aloud] You arrive in the bustling market town of Dragon Thorpe. You have few provisions except for a purse containing a few gold pieces. It is late in the evening, and you head towards the town's tavern hoping to find accommodation for the night. You enter the tavern and head across to the fireplace to warm yourself. You see the innkeeper busily serving drinks and meals to punters. A few weary-looking souls are heading upstairs. Perhaps there is accommodation here? What do you do next?

- Meet the other players/NPCs and agree on plans for your campaign.
- Buy food and ale, served by the innkeeper at the bar to replenish a hit point (cost 1 treasure piece). [Read aloud] *"Aye, we can fix you up with*

a meal and a flagon of the good stuff, take a seat my friends."

- Buy a night's lodgings at the inn. The inn keeper charges 2 gold pieces. A good night's rest will restore one hit point. [Read aloud] *"Yes good sirs, we can put you up for the night. That'll be two gold pieces. Certainly, beats camping out in the cold night air!"*

- Interact with other non-player characters. [Read aloud] You approach some of the locals to engage in conversation out of politeness, but you soon realise that they are uncouth ruffians, who are very drunk. On each occasion, conversation leads to drunken conflict, and you have to use your charisma to deflate the situation.

- If players interact with the locals, they must make a charisma ability test [5] to avoid a fight. Otherwise create a non-player character to fight with (e.g., use the orc stat block). If a player chooses to make a wisdom test [5], one of the drunks confides to them [Read aloud] *"I'm the town's gravedigger. I hate the job, like. Folks' recon there's a powerful spell book in the tomb at the graveyard containing a curse. I dare not go in to find out. The place is haunted for sure."*

- Interact with another character, [Read aloud] *"This place was called Riverthorpe in the good old days, before that awful dragon came. It was he who killed the old mage in the tower over the river, you know."*

- Spend the night in the tavern to rest and recover. [Read aloud] The innkeeper leads you to the lodgings rooms upstairs. There are several tatty beds, and you choose the ones that look cleanest to spend the night in. You set down your accoutrements and close your eyes. The tavern is more comfortable than the wilderness, but you are restless, as you are aware of the eyes on you from the inscrutable fellow with whom you share the lodgings. What do you do next?

- Leave the tavern and camp outside in the cold (-1 hit point).
- Remain in the tavern and rest (+1 hit point). You must make a wisdom test [10] in order to remain aware of the thief otherwise you are attacked by a thief, needing a dexterity saving throw of [12] to avoid the surprise attack.

Encounter 2 – The Marketplace

[Read aloud] You stroll back into town and head towards the marketplace. The market is a hive of activity with people trading and bartering goods, such as weapons, armour and foodstuffs. The market at Dragon Thorpe is a great place to purchase equipment and provisions. However, be vigilant. There are numerous thieves and thugs in the marketplace looking for an opportunity to rob the stallholders. What do you do?

- Purchase weapon upgrades such as the artisan long sword or barbarian battle-axe (+3 to your STR attack roll, price 20 gold).
- Purchase foodstuffs to replace a lost hit point (1 gold piece).
- Steal upgrades – Players can behave as thugs and steal one item from the stall holders. They will need a dexterity ability roll of DEX [20] to test sleight of hand, otherwise they get caught.

[Read aloud] As you try to steal the item, the stallholder catches you in the act. He alerts the town sheriff, and you are chased out of town and never allowed to return. You may not come back to the market or tavern if caught stealing.

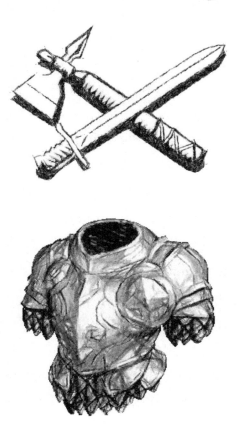

Encounter 3 – Exhuming the Dead

[Read aloud] You arrive at the graveyard and approach the tomb. Inside, you see a solitary stone coffin lit up by the glow of a shrine on the far wall, which emits a hazy green light. You decide to explore the tomb. What do you do?

- Roll intelligence [10] to see if you remember anything from your conversations in the tavern: [Read aloud] *"According to the fellow in the tavern, the spell book is somewhere in this tomb."*
- Observe the shrine and read the writings on the shrine: [Read aloud] You study the shrine and, in the dim, green light you see that there is writing in the stonework. It says that the spell book is hidden within the tomb of a deceased sorcerer. He was the former resident in the mage's tower. The spells in this book are believed to grant extraordinary magical powers

and evil curses. Below this message, there are a series of demonic-looking icons, which glow strongly with the green energy.

- Open the coffin – [Read aloud] Believing that the spell book would fetch a fair price on the Black Market, you open the coffin. A ray of green energy bursts forth to reveal a pile of bones amongst which the spell book and a gleaming sword are buried. What do you do?

- Leave the book where it is and exit the tomb.

- Reach for the book/sword: [Read aloud] You lean over the coffin, the green light coming from the bones lights up your face. The instant that you touch the book, a skeleton warrior manifests itself from the pile of bones and attacks! What do you do?

- Fight the skeleton – a new skeleton emerges from the coffin after each one is defeated. The only way to stop the spell is to smash the shrine containing the demonic symbols (AC=18, two players can combine their rolls to reach this number). After the events play out, [Read aloud] You smash the demonic shrine, and the green glow disappears. Amidst the blackness, you grab the spell book from the coffin and hastily retreat.

- Read from the book. [Read aloud] the spells contained within the book contain the magic incantations needed to infuse potions with transformative power. While browsing the pages, you notice one section titled "Metamorphosis: dragons."

The Dungeon

About this adventure

[Read aloud] You enter the dungeon in search of the fabled treasure belonging to "the beast", who is said to be half man and half monster. The treasure is rumoured to be contained in the depths of the labyrinth. Few adventurers are brave enough to enter this haunted abode, but the rewards may be well worth the risk.

- [DM note] Dungeon chambers are made up from 8x11 grids on A4 sheets, which you can find/make online, and are shown in schematics to inform the lay out.
- You can choose to sketch out the terrain features to resemble the schematics, or some players prefer to carefully craft 3d terrain pieces.
- There is also a schematic of the dungeon layout to indicate where the chambers are relative to one another and to help you keep an eye on where abouts in the dungeons the adventurers are positioned.

Image of rooms layout

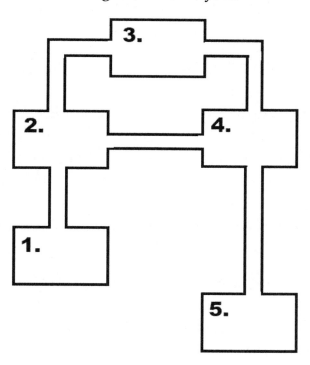

Encounter 1 – The Collapsed Corridor

[Read aloud] You have arrived at the dungeon seeking the treasures rumoured to be located within. The fortress is in a state of disrepair and many of the walls are in ruins. You enter inside the dungeon via a collapsed corridor. Rubble is piled to the left and scattered across the floor. The ceiling is scarcely held up by six pillars, which are precariously leaning inwards towards the centre of the corridor.

At the far side of the corridor, you find the gatekeeper, an ogre, guarding a locked door into the chamber beyond. He asks in a guttural voice, "why have you come?"

- Trick the ogre – (CHA [14] needed to test your charisma). With a successful lie, players convince the ogre to let them inside. With a failed lie, he attacks.
- Slay the ogre and search for keys. [Read aloud] On the ogre's dead body, you find the keys to the locked door.

- Knock down the door. This will require a strength roll STR [14]. Falling rubble, beware. [Read aloud] The room begins to tremble and the ceiling collapses. Rubble falls and large pieces of masonry crash upon the floor. Then the pillars shake and tumble inwardly causing the ceiling to cave in at the centre of the corridor. All who were stood in the centre of the corridor now lay dead, buried in the rubble.
- Players can kill the ogre this way by knocking down the pillars STR [5] so that the roof collapses onto the ogre but ensure that there are no characters stood in the middle of the columns when the roof falls in!

Map of encounter 1

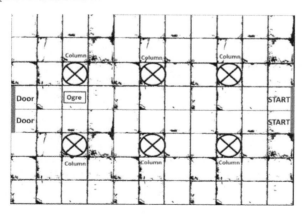

Encounter 2 – The Haunted Hall

[Read aloud] You pass through the collapsed corridor and into another lofty hall containing six, albeit sturdier, pillars. The hallway is dark, being dimly lit by two lanterns above the entrance door. The ghosts of ancient warriors linger in the dark halls away from the torchlight of the lanterns. Through the gloom, you can make out a fountain on the far wall. There is also a piece of furniture along the side of the hall opposite a door. What do you want to do?

- Head down the hall. [Read aloud] As the ghosts pass by, you feel they cause you harm. To pass through the hall, take a CON saving throw [17] to avoid taking d4 damage.
- Grab the lantern and use it to guide your way safely through the hall.
- Investigate the enchanted mirror, or the fountain, or the curious door.

The enchanted mirror

[Read aloud] After travelling down the long corridor, you arrive at something interesting. There is a huge frame concealed by an old blanket inviting you to look at it. What do you do?

- Pull off the blanket to look at what is underneath – [Read aloud] You pull down the blanket to find that the frame contains a mirror. This is no ordinary mirror because, instead of seeing your own reflection, you see an image of a monster that is half man and half bull wandering in a room full of piles of treasure.
- Smash the mirror – [DM note] the mirror contains an enchantment spell protecting the minotaur in encounter 5 by reducing the adventurers attacks by one half.

The possessed fountain

[Read aloud] The fountain decorating the far wall dominates the room and is apparently used for drinking water. Besides this water feature, the chamber is evidently unused, judging from the cobwebs covering the alcoves between the fountain and the columns. What do you want to do?

- Investigate the fountain – [Read aloud] On the fountains edge, there is a brass cup, used for drinking, presumably. Water is spilling over the lip of the fountain and leaking into a lower chamber somewhere. You peer into the waters of the fountain and find that some jewels have been dropped in along with a large brass key.

- Use the cup to get a drink of water. The water is refreshing and restores +2 hit points.
- Reach into the fountain to retrieve the jewels and/or key. [Read aloud] You dip your hand into the water and snatch the items. As you pocket the trinkets, a ghost manifests above the fountain and then attacks you.
- [DM note] the key is for the door to the minotaur chamber.
- Investigate the cobwebs – [Read aloud] Among the cobwebs, you stumble across an old chest. Before you get a chance to investigate it, a skeleton drops out from the cobwebs. Animated with a perverse lifeforce, it attacks you.
- Note the chest contains 10 gold pieces if the players open it.

The curious door

[Read aloud] You arrive at a curious door at the end of the corridor. It contains the insignia of a bull upon it above the brass door handles. A long-dead knight is slumped next to it.

- Try the door. It is locked and cannot be broken down.
- Search the knight to find a brass key (belonging to the door).
- The key from the fountain doesn't fit this door.
- Listen at the door: you hear the noise of footsteps in the next room.
- Unlock the door and go through (encounter 4): find an orc; it issues a surprise attack if players don't listen at the door first. This means that the orc takes a hit against the first player through the door, without needing to make a STR roll first.

Map of encounter 2

Encounter 3 – Into the Sewers

Mirky pool

[Read aloud] You find yourself at the top of a stairs leading down into another chamber, with a doorway at the far side up another flight of stairs. The room is flooded across its full width, with a deep mirky pool, but otherwise empty. Water leaking from the walls continues to flood the chamber. What do you do?

- Walk through the pool – the players are affected by the cold water and must make a constitution saving throw CON [18] to avoid having to take d4 damage. The first player to enter the water is attacked by a constrictor snake. [Read aloud]: You enter the cold, cold water and feel a shiver run through your body like lighting. The leader of your group, while shivering, suddenly screams out for help. A large constrictor snake has coiled around their leg in the pool.
- Fight the snake.
- Search the mirky pool – the pool is divided into 6 sections. Each section contains a different artifact, indicated in the table below. However, there are more constrictor snakes in the pool.

DM to roll a d6 and if the score corresponds to a section of the pool containing an adventurer, they are attacked i.e., you roll a "2" so an adventure in section 2 is attacked.

1.	Ancient sword (+3) attack.
2.	Two phials of healing potion.
3.	Gauntlets of Strength (+3) to STR rolls.
4.	Armour chest plate +2 AC.
5.	Old boots (+2-inch movement when worn).
6.	Three snake eggs (restore +3 HP when eaten).

Flood

[DM note] There is a time limit to be in this chamber of **6** turns before the chamber floods and the players must escape. [Read aloud] As you investigate the pool, more and more water leaks from the walls, there is a rumble, and a torrent of water spills forth into the chamber and it begins to fill.

• After the players have taken their first turn, read out the flood caption. Players must get up one of the staircases to safety in **6** turns, before the chamber floods and they drown. But beware, of being held up by a snake!

Map of encounter 3

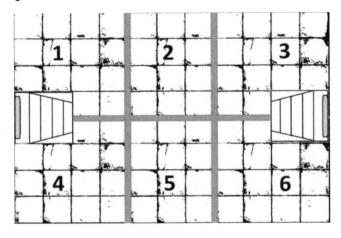

Encounter 4 – The Perilous Platform

[Read aloud] You move on into the next chamber. At the opposite side of the room, there is another doorway which contains the same insignia as the curious door in the haunted hall. This door is stationed on a raised platform that is four stone flags wide and four stone flags long, making it stand out from the other doors in the dungeon. There is nothing valuable noticeable in the room, but it is nevertheless guarded by an orc.

- If players have listened at the curious door, then they should be prepared for the orc. If they announce their entrance (e.g., knock on the door, or call out), then the orc does not attack. [Read aloud] Upon your entrance to the chamber, he shouts "Hey you, what business have you being here?"
- Negotiate with the orc – attempt to persuade the orc that you are just lost, and quickly leave the room. CHA test [15]. Bribe him with 10 gold to let you through the door with the insignia upon

it, CHA [16]. Tell the orc that you are treasure traders and would like to see what is stored in the dungeon CHA [18].

- Fight the orc. A search of his dead body reveals a transcript, which has the following written upon it: [Read aloud] "The traps on the platform will stop you dead to secure the treasures that lay ahead. Here is the safest route to go forth and see the loot." Then there is a list of numbers as follows (1,3); (2,3); (3,3); (3,2); (3,1); (2,1). [DM note] these are the coordinates for the safe route through the traps on the raised platform. Players should be left to figure this out after you write down the list of coordinates for them.

- The traps take d6 damage if a player crosses one.

- Open the door on the platform – it is locked. Players need the key from the possessed fountain. The door cannot be opened by any other means.

Map of encounter 4

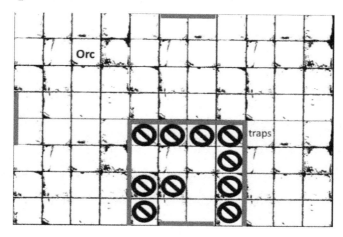

Encounter 5 – Escaping the Treasury

[Read aloud] The curious door on the platform opens to a narrow stairway. You head down it to the next chamber. Finally, you have arrived at the treasury. Piles of gold are heaped up across the floor. You are tempted to head over to the piles of gold and start filling your pockets. What do you do?

- [DM note] A minotaur patrols this room. It has a fixed circuit between the treasure heaps, indicated on the dungeon map. It moves sequentially from position 1, 2, 3... on each monster's turn. If the adventurers are in line of sight when the minotaur appears, it attacks. However, keep the miniature off the table until it bumps into the players, so that they can't trace its route easily. Players must set a look-out to alert the others when it is coming. Use a d6 dice to keep track of the minotaur's route.

- One player can listen/look out for the minotaur. A WIZ test [12] enables you to determine if it approaches by the *sound of footsteps*, otherwise the minotaur will appear without warning and attack. When alerted to the beast's arrival, players can move off around another corner, or choose to hide behind some terrain scenery with a DEX stealth test of [10].

- Collect treasure – players can collect 5 gold per turn and collect a maximum of 50 gold each in this treasury, which will depend on how many turns they stay in the dungeon for.

- Fight the minotaur – remember, it has an enchantment spell on it from the mirror, which means that attacks must be reduced by one half, unless the mirror is broken.

- Escape the treasury with the looted treasure. Players can decide to leave the dungeon at any time with the treasure that they have collected. If you are playing a campaign, it might come in useful in the future!

Map of encounter 5

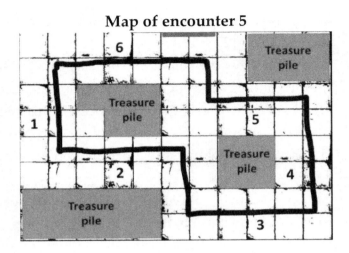

The Necromancer's Tower

About this adventure

This adventure builds on the storyline from *Wandering the Wild Woods*, which was the first part of this adventure, where you meet the wizard in the tower. However, things are no longer as they were...

The town, called Dragon Thorpe, has since become known as Old Town, after it was ruined by the dragon, overrun by monsters from the dungeon and deserted by the townsfolk. The mage in the tower is rumoured to be known as the "necromancer" having the ability to raise the dead. Perhaps he can be of help to restore your lost comrades on this adventure?

[Read aloud] You arrive at the necromancer's tower seeking his help to restore a lost friend. As you approach the tower, you are greeted by the old mage himself, who shouts down to you from the roof of the tower, "Friends, friends, how can I be of service to you? The door is open come on in. In return for my help, though, you must complete a task for me at each level of the tower. Only then will I return your friend from the netherworld."

[DM notes] Regarding set-up, the mage's tower consists of five single-room stories with a set of stairs to a door leading up to each room. The rooms are filled with generic apothecary furniture, such as desks, bookcases, crates, barrels, chests etc. and specific furnishings might be described in the scenario. So, set up a room for each encounter that fits this description, using the picture below as a guide, and add the relevant encounter-specific features as you get to them.

Schematic of a room in the mage's tower (encounters will also need to include specific objects).

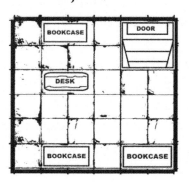

Encounter 1 – The Caustic Cauldron

[Read aloud] You enter the necromancer's tower at the bottom level through the open door that leads into the potion brewery. The tower is constructed from five stories, each is a single room containing a set of stairs that leads up to the next level.

You notice that the door to the first floor is blocked with iron bars. In the centre of the room, there is a large cauldron bubbling away. Clearly the mage has been busy brewing potions made from the variety of accoutrements that clutter the shelves and desks in the room.

[DM notes] the challenge for the players is to brew a caustic potion for the mage. Incidentally, this can be used to melt the iron bars and gain access to level 2. The room set-up contains a cauldron at the centre and shelves and a desk around the edges of the room that contain the items needed to brew the potion.

- Investigate the cauldron – the large black cauldron contains a green fluid that is bubbling violently above a hot fire.

- Investigate the desks – among the assorted parchments you find a leather-bound book titled "Brewers Guide to Caustic Potions" with a long red bookmark placed a third of the way in the text.

- Open the book at the marked page and read: "A caustic brew to melt metal through; add the ingredients in correct proportion to avoid harm to you. Add the ingredients in numbers square, starting with one weasel, or else beware! Here are the ingredients for this potion: weasel, snake eggs, bats wings, toadstools, dead bugs, to be added in correct proportions to avoid commotion." [DM note] that these ingredients are added in proportion based on square numbers, 1, 4, 9, 16, and 25 respectively. See table for details.

- Investigate the shelves – the shelves are full of miscellaneous items, such as scriptures, potion bottles and animal parts. You will have to search keenly to find anything specific: WIZ [10] search action (see table). The players will search different shelves, bookcases and desk surfaces etc and will discover the items in the following order:

Item 1 – you find a dead weasel, dried out and odour free.
Item 2 – you find a half dozen snake eggs (DM: only 4 to be added to potion. The remaining 2 can be eaten to gain +1 HP.)
Item 3 – you find a jar containing a dozen dried bat wings. (DM: only 9 required).
Item 4 – you find a small sack that is full of toadstools (DM: poisonous if eaten d4 damage; 16 needed for potion).
Item 5 – you find a large jar that is full to the brim with dead beetles. (DM: 25 to be added.)

- Note that if the ingredients are added in the wrong proportions the potion bubbles more violently and splashes the players, causing d4 damage, each time players make a mistake. The potion will still work if the proportions of ingredients are wrong, as long as they have all been added. [Read aloud] You finish adding the final ingredients to the potion. The bubbling stops and it is ready for use.

Encounter 2 – Let There Be Light

[Read aloud] You get through the barred door and enter the next room, which is lit with a red glow. The room appears to be some kind of herbarium, with miscellaneous plants positioned about the room; most noticeably are some carnivorous plants that look somewhat familiar to you. Inconveniently, one of them is positioned by the stairway to the next door, impeding your access to the next level. What do you do?

- Fight the plant (use stats for awakened tree)
- Investigate the room – during your search of the room, you find a note written by the mage, which says, "Remember to prune the flesh-feasters" and you also discover three coloured crystals placed upon trestles. One is red, one is blue and the other yellow. The red one is positioned in front of the window and is the source of the red glow. [DM note] blue + yellow makes green when placed in front of the window to calm the plants, so that players can get past and open the door.

- Make an intelligence roll to see what you know about these plants INT [12] – [read aloud] you remember that you have read about these plants in a book and know that, under red light, the plants are very aggressive, and under green light, they are calm.

Encounter 3 – A Box of Boggarts

[Read aloud] You enter the next room of the tower, which appears to be the mage's study. In the middle of the room, there are four large chests. What do you want to do?

[DM note] Three Boggarts (ghost stats) haunt 3 of the chests, and alternate between the chests, meaning that a different one is safe each turn. The safe chest follows the order 1, 3, 2, 4 changing on each monster's turn. Keep track using a die to count which of the four chests is safe. Note on a sketch map which chest corresponds to each number e.g., are they number 1-4 from left to right?

- Open a chest – [read aloud] you lift the lid of the chest, and a boggart appears from inside and hovers above the chest, guarding its contents. It does not attack (unless players try to grab the item). The chest contains:

Chest 1 – contains a gold ring (when worn, the ring of immortality enables you to communicate with the dead).
Chest 2 – contains a large brass key (for the door).
Chest 3 – contains a pair of old spectacles (when worn, the spectacles show hidden objects).
Chest 4 – contains an incense burner (when lit, can be used to ward off spirits, using the specific command word "purgatory").

- DM: do not tell players about the actions that these items perform, as they must figure this out to get through the door.

The door to level 4

[Read aloud] You approach the door and try the handle, but it will not open. You wonder if it is locked but cannot find a keyhole.

- [DM note] the door is haunted by another boggart. A player wearing the ring of immortality is able to communicate with him.
- Communicate with the boggart – [read aloud] You put on the ring and suddenly see the

boggart who guards the door. Noticing that you are able to perceive him, he addresses you, "speak the command word while making fumes to send me away to my abode and grant yourself passage through this door, or I shall attack you."

- When lit, the incense burner can be used to ward off spirits, using the specific command word "purgatory." An INT test [12] enables the player to successfully guess the command word.
- The keyhole is hidden with a spell but can be seen if the old spectacles are worn. Player can then place the key in the right place and unlock the door.

Encounter 4 – Where Did He Leave the Keys?

[Read aloud] You move up to level four and walk past six barrels in the room towards the door. However, this time it is most apparent that the door is locked because there are six large padlocks on it, preventing you from opening it.

[DM notes] Door has 6 padlocks on it that can't be picked. The keys are in the bottom of the barrels. Players are to open the barrels to find what's in them. This includes one key and an obstacle. Players can use the contents of each barrel to destroy a challenge contained in another barrel (see table below for details). The barrels are pre-labelled, if the players care to take a WIZ test [8].

Acid Fog   Insect Swarm   Gold

Storm   Snake   Rat

Table of barrel contents

Barrel 1. Acid fog (causes d4 damage each turn until removed using contained storm to blow fumes away.)
Barrel 2. Swarm of insects (kill using acid fog)
Barrel 3. Contains 10 gold, but you step on a hinge trap (DEX [17] to undo, d4 damage each attempt.
Barrel 4. Contained storm (blows a strong wind that can blow away acid fog. Causes -1 HP damage).
Barrel 5. Giant snake (use hinge trap to capture it.)
Barrel 6. Giant rat (giant snake to capture it).

- The acid fog comes out of barrel 1, each player takes d4 damage on every turn taken after the barrel is open. To reach the key inside, the player must take d4 damage. The fumes can be used to kill the swarm of insects. The fumes can be blown away by opening barrel 4, labelled "contained storm".

- The swarm of insects leaves barrel 2 when a player collects the key. They can either fight against the insects or open the acid fog barrel for one turn (taking d4 damage) and kill the insects in one turn.

- Barrel 3, containing gold and a key, is trapped. To search for the trap needs WIZ [18] to find it, then a DEX [17] to disarm it, causing d4 damage on each failed attempt. When disarmed, it can be used to capture either the giant snake or the giant rat, when the creature escapes their barrel. Note that the snake will catch the rat. Players will have to fight these creatures, if a trap is not used.

- Barrel 4 contains a storm spell, causing -1 HP damage when the lid is opened. The storm can be used to blow away the fog, so that the players can open barrel 1 without incurring any further harm.

- [DM note] If players put on the ring of immortality, they find the last of the boggarts in the room. A CHA [14] roll convinces it to help with the challenge, and it states to the adventurers: "the contents of one barrel may be used to overcome the challenges found in another."

- Once all six keys are collected from the barrels, the door can be opened.

Encounter 5 – It's Like Talking to a Door

[Read aloud] You enter the highest room of the tower. It is full of generic furniture, such as shelving, tables and chairs etc. and there appears to be no obstacles to overcome in order to pass through the final door at the top of the stairs leading to the roof, where the mage, presumably, is still stood, observing the lands around Dragon Thorpe from atop of the tower.

[DM note] Players take their first turn and can explore the room, or head straight for the door. When they try the door, [read aloud] the moment you touch the doorknob, a face appears from the woodwork and addresses you by saying, "answer my riddles correctly to gain passage to the mage."

- Riddle 1 – "A lustrous metal of great worth, hard to find in the earth. Its yellow shine, makes jewellery fine." [gold].
- Riddle 2 – "A serpent on wings who knows many things, has the power to burn villages and smite kings." [dragon].

- Riddle 3 – "What crows at dawn, scratches the farmer's lawn, does not lay eggs but from eggs is born?" [Cockerill/rooster].

- Riddle 4 – "Its pale face is seen in the dark and hides again come the song of a lark. Then it appears again the next night, not always the same shape, not always the same light." [moon].

- Riddle 5 – "Fluid of the fang can cause a pang. You it shall smite if a snake will bite. What is this? [venom].

- Riddle 6 – "A riddle for each door, a dozen by half. Take this number and chant it by three. Tell me the code to exit this abode by telling me the number three times. What is the pass code to pass this door?" [666].

Encounter 6 – Meeting the Mage

[Read aloud] Finally, after a series of challenging encounters to meet his acquaintance, you arrive at the roof of the tower to speak with the mage. He offers to help you, provided you help him with some gruelling missions. "If you go to Old Town and help rid it of monsters, I will restore your friend from the dead. I would start however, by destroying Shiba the giant spider who plagues the realm. While you're there. Collect her venom for my apothecary and I will reward you well."

Webs of Woe

[Read aloud] You have been chosen to get rid of the creatures plagueing Old Town starting with the giant spider, named Shiba, who resides in the caves in the hills. You enter the spider's lair. Stone columns hold up the roof of the cave, formed from years of water erosion. You light your torches because, ahead of you, there is a menacing darkness hiding Shiba, the most loathsome monster in Old Town.

[DM note] numbers designate the positions of webs in the cave. If a player touches a web, the spider comes and attacks. A single successful hit will send the spider cawarding away. It retreats and comes back again the next time that one of the webs is disturbed. Each numbered web is also associated with an encounter for the players to tackle.

About this adventure – the tile set-up is made of 2xA4 dungeon tiles next to each other and contains x8 3x3 stone columns that support the roof of the cave on to which the dreadful webs are attached. Players must traverse this cave and hunt the giant spider, while avoiding the harmful webs.

Map of the caves

Encounter 1

[Read aloud] You light your torches and enter the cave, home to Shiba, the giant spider. Every knuck and cranny is cluttered with cobwebs. The path ahead is cluttered with webs across the width of the cave all the way from the ceiling to a couple of feet from the floor, obstructing your passage. What do you do?

- Crawl under the net of webs.
- Cut through them, which disturbs the spider and it attacks.

- Push through them – you become entangled STR [14] to escape before the spider arrives.

Encounter 2

[Read aloud] Around the corner, you observe a skeleton, tangled in webs, hanging from the ceiling. Among the tattered rags of clothing, you notice a gold necklace around its neck. What do you do?

- Trapped – DEX [12] to obtain the necklace without losing 1 HP. Necklace is worth 20 gold + players disturb the spider.
- Leave the skeleton and necklace and move on.

Encounter 3

[Read aloud] Cobwebs clutter the next alcove in the cave. However, they are not as thick here, and with care, it would be possible to sneak through them without touching them. Among them, you espy a chest. What do you do?

- DEX [14] to approach the chest without alerting the giant spider, Shiba. Chest contains 10 gold and an old lantern.
- Leave the chest and move on.

Encounter 4

[Read aloud] In this corner of the cave, which is also cluttered in cobwebs, you find a sword anchored into a crack in the cave ceiling. What do you want to do?

- Investigate the sword, avoiding touching the cobwebs and alerting the giant spider DEX [12].
- Collect sword – to move it requires STR [14] and causes a cave-in [read aloud] as you wrestle with the anchored sword, you loosen some rock fragments in the cave ceiling and they fall to the floor. DEX [12] to avoid taking d6 damage.

Encounter 5

[Read aloud] You continue your journey through the cave, led by the light of your flaming torches. The light disturbes a swarm of bats and they swirl and flutter in the tunnel ahead.

- Disturb a swarm of bats – fight them to carry on in this direction.
- Move away from the swarm.

Encounter 6

[Read aloud] A poisonous black gas lingers in the tunnel ahead. You can't see even with torches lit, what do you do?

- CON [14] to avoid its poisenous effects (d6 damage otherwise).
- Returnt to encounter 5,
- or move to encounter 7, disturbing the webs and spider as you pass through blinded by the black gas. Spider gets a surprise attack on the first player.

Encounter 7

[Read aloud] You enter a differernt region of the tunnel network and a gust of wind blows down the tunnel straight through you and causes your torches to be put out.

- Gust of wind blows out torches. Players can either light the lantern and use it, or try and get to the next encounter in the dark WIZ [14]. Players are at a disadvantage in fighting the spider when they walk into webs, roll d20 twice and use lowest score for the battle STR roll.

Encounter 8

[Read aloud] You have arrived at the spiders nest and must fight Shiba to the death. She sits on her bed of webs watching you, and the moment that you approach too close, she jerks forwards and attacks.

- Fight spider, engaging in combat.
- Throw flaming lantern onto the webs and burn the giant spider DEX [16] for accuracy, but must return from the cave in the dark, requiring WIZ [14] to avoid becoming trapped in the webs and completely lost.

The Ruins of Old Town

About this adventure: Part 1

The adventurers are given a mission to retrieve a necklace from Old Town, formerly known as Dragon Thorpe, which has become overrun with monsters. They're going to have to be quick, because in part 2 of this adventure, the monsters turn hostile.

[Read aloud to the adventurers]

You head into Old Town searching for the princess' necklace. She is rightful heir to the kingdom and has been put under a sleeping spell by a witch. The only way to reverse the spell is to place her necklace on her, so that the kingdom can be reclaimed. This is your mission, to find the lost diamond necklace at return home with it.

Map of Old Town

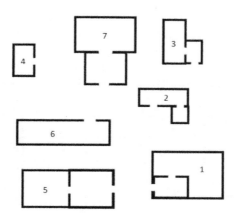

Building 1 – The Haunted Monastery

Map of the monastery

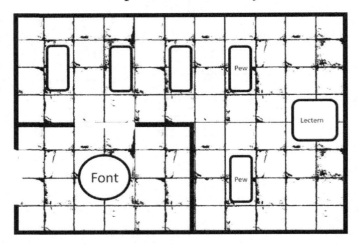

Encounter 1 – by the font.

[Read aloud] Inside the foyer of the monastery, you see the font containing the holy water that was used by the communion to cleanse themselves before heading inside for prayers. There is also a large chest in the corner of the room. What do you want to do?

- Note that the font containing holy water can be drank to restore +1 hit point (HP) and/or collected for protection against demonic spirits.
- The door to the congregation is locked – note that the key is in the chest. Players can boot the door in with a strength STR test [15] to break open the heavy oaken doors.
- Open the chest - The chest contains old garments and nothing apparently of value. However, a search action with a WIZ test of [8] enables players to find the key in a coat pocket (or specifically players may state that they checked the coat pockets) along with a note saying, "Satan has captured the monastery. Only The holy book may protect you here!"

Encounter 2 – in the congregation.

[Read aloud] Inside the main hall of the monastery, you find rows of empty pews. As you walk down the aisle towards the lectern, a ghost manifests from the ether and attacks you.

- Players are in a combat encounter with the ghost. See appendix 4 for the stat block for fighting a ghost. Note that players might think to head towards the lectern and collect the bible from there, which can be used to ward off the evil spirit and avoid the combat encounter. (Note that a clue to this was given in the note in encounter 1 and an intelligence INT test of [12] will enable the DM to tell the players that this is a good idea).

Encounter 3 – in the graveyard.

[Read aloud] You leave the monastery through the graveyard and head on the path back into the town square. You notice that some of the graves contain stones with an inverted cross on them, a sign of evil. Do you want to investigate these or come back later?

[Read aloud] One of the graves you come across belongs to a witch. On the gravestone it says, "the wicked witch was buried with her wealth, earned as blood money from her craft." What do you want to do.

- Players can dig up the corpse of the witch to look for her treasure. [read aloud] You exhume the witch and collect 100 gold pieces from the coffin. However, the moment you pocked the coins, her eyes open and she attacks. Note that the witch is immune to attacks, players must douse the witch in holy water to vanquish her.

Building 2 – The Blacksmith's Workshop

Map of the workshop

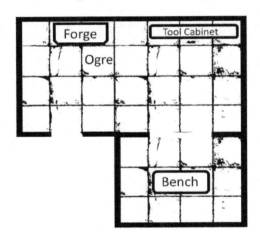

Encounter 1 – the ogre's smithy.

[Read aloud] Inside the blacksmiths forge, you find an ogre busily hammering iron on an anvil. Your intrusion angers him and he attacks you.

- A combat encounter with the ogre (see appendix 4 for details).

- Once the ogre is dead, player will be able to search the room. The door to the backroom is locked and is a heavy metal door that cannot be broken into. Player can use the blacksmith's tools and forge to break through the door and get into the backroom.

Encounter 2 – the backroom.

[Read aloud] Using the blacksmith's tools, you break the hinges on the door and the heavy iron door falls inwards into the backroom. Inside you find a workbench laden with weapons, the blacksmiths finest and rare crafts.

- Players collect rare armour +3 to AC, and a rare longsword, +3 to attack rolls.

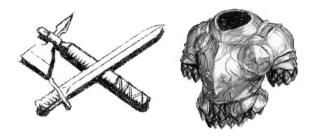

Building 3 – The Town Sewers

Map of the sewers

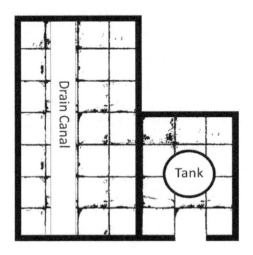

Encounter 1 – down the drain.

[Read aloud] Inside the outbuilding, you find the tank leading to the sewers underground. The tank is lined with excrement and a pungent smell emanates from within. What do you want to do?

- Leave the smelly building or take a CON test [8] to avoid -1 HP damage from the poisonous fumes coming from the tank.

- Climb down the tank into the sewers below. players will need to collect a length of rope to do this.

Encounter 2 – in the sewers.

[Read aloud] Inside the sewers you find the place heaving with rats, all running along the length of the drain canal. Down here, the smell is even worse (take a CON [10] test). What do you want to do?

- Search in the drain canal for useful items – as the players rummage among the sewerage, they are attacked by a swarm of rats. After fighting off the rats, they find the diamond necklace belonging to the princess.

Building 4 – The Hag's Hovel

Map of the hovel

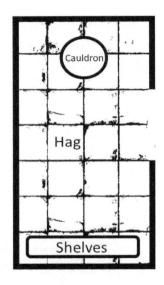

Encounter 1 – the cauldron by the fire.

[Read aloud] Inside the hag's hovel, you find the old woman hunched over a cauldron by the fire. At the other side of the room are shelves filled with ingredients that she adds to the cauldron. What do you want to do?

- Talk to the hag – players can ask questions pertaining to the potion. The hag can brew a healing potion to cure all HP, or brew poison. DM to roll a dice (odd vs even) to determine which it is.
- Players can try to charm the hag to give some of the healing potion, but this doesn't work. Intimidation must be used CHA [10] to get some of the potion, but there is 50/50 risk of being poisoned and death.
- Players can slay the hag (use goblin stats for combat) and take the potion.
- Players can start a new potion using the ingredients on the shelves if they search them (WIZ test [9]) and find the healing potion recipe on the shelf.

Building 5 – The Town Prison

Map of the prison

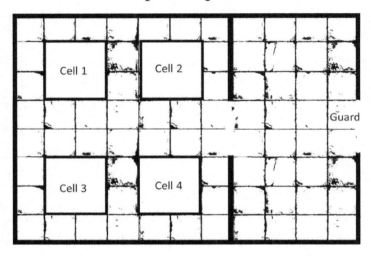

Encounter 1 – the guardhouse.

[Read aloud] You arrive at the town prison and are greeted at the door by the guardsman. He looks shifty and crooked and frankly, like he belongs in the jail, not guarding it. He says to you, "Halt! What business have you here?" what do you want to do?

- Talk with the guard – players can talk with the guard in an attempt to gain entry. Options include tell a lie or use intimidation to gain passage (CHA test [16]) or pay him a bribe with 50 gold.

- Engage in combat (use orc stats) – players can slay the guard but must discard the body somewhere (the sewer tank) in the next encounter to avoid aggravating the townsfolk/monsters on Old Town. [Read aloud] You wipe the guard's blood from your weapons, and you hear a voice cry out "You killed the guard, I'm off to tell the sheriff," and the goblin scurries off before you can accost him. You are in trouble now! What do you want to do?

- If the player who killed the guard fails to discard the corpse, that player is locked in the jail and must be rescued using the keys stored by the sheriff of Old Town in a secret place in the townhouse.

Encounter 2 – the jail.

[Read aloud] Inside the jail room, you find four cells containing prisoners. They appear to be peasant folk from the surrounding settlements.

Upon your entry, they plead for help. What do you want to do?

- Talk to the prisoners – The frail old men say to you, "find the keys and let us out and we'll gift you a diamond necklace" …
- [Read aloud] You rescue the prisoners and find out that the princess' necklace was thrown into the sewer by the princess when monsters came to steal it. You must go and get it.

Building 6 – The Townhouse

Map of the townhouse

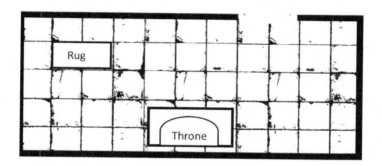

Encounter 1 – the townhouse.

[Read aloud] You step inside the townhouse to have an audience with the sheriff of Old Town, who is revealed to be a minotaur, sitting upon a throne in the building. Besides the ornamented chair, you notice a decorative rug on the floor and a fantastic tapestry on the wall. As you approach the throne, the beast calls out to you, "Who are you travellers that march in here uninvited, tell me about yourselves at once!"

- Talk with the minotaur – players can decide to answer the troll. CHA test [8] to avoid angering him with your answer.
- Combat the minotaur.
- Search under the rug to find a trapdoor to a cellar full of valuables worth 100 gold.
- Search behind the tapestry to find a wall safe. Inside are a set of four keys on a ring (these are for the jail cells, but do not tell the players where they fit).

Building 7 – The Tavern

Map of the tavern

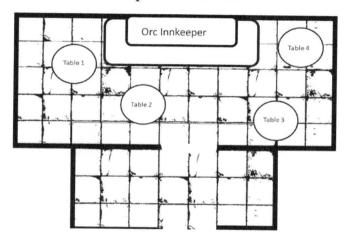

Encounter 1 – the bar.

[Read aloud] You head through the porch and head inside the tavern and walk up to the bar. The innkeeper is an orc and reticently asks how he can be of service. What do you want to do?

- Talk with the barkeep – players can talk with the bar keep. They can order a beer which restores 1 HP and costs 5 gold, multiple beers can be bought, but take a CON test [5, 10, 15, 20] for each consecutive pint to avoid being drunk and sitting out the next encounter.

- Talk with the orcs at the tavern tables. They can sell useful items such as a length of rope, 10 gold, weapons +1 to attack rolls, 10 gold. DM will have to improvise the roll-playing a bit here.

About this adventure: Part 2

[Read aloud] You arrive at the ruins of Old Town. Formerly known as Dragon Thorpe, now forgotten town that was deserted after the desolation caused by a terrifying red dragon, whose fiery breath burnt the town almost to the ground. Now, only charred ruins remain. It is rumoured that treasures or valuable trinkets may be present in the ruined buildings, left behind by those who fled the dragon's wrath. However, no one has ever dared search the ruins of Old Town because a rabble of monsters now frequent there, ready to attack any unwary adventurers who are brave enough to set foot in the ruins of Old Town.

[DM notes] This adventure is designed to be similar to a skirmish game. The objective of the game is to go into the ruined Old Town and search the dilapidated buildings for treasures and useful trinkets that might come in handy for future adventures and slay the monsters that habituate there. The game set-up will be on a larger map than usual D&D encounters to represent the whole town, and include carefully crafted terrain pieces, such as ruined buildings to liven-up the game (conversely you could just mark-out the plans for the building footprints on a battle map, if you don't have time for crafting.

Table of search encounters

Options	Outcomes
Doors, windows, and other entrances	• Trapped • Barred • Open
Chests, barrels, and crates	1. Empty 2. Trapped 3. Locked 4. Creature 5. Portal key 6. Treasure
Traps!	• Hidden (search) WIZ [15] • Disarm DEX [15] • Set traps
Treasure!	1. Gold 2. Healing potion 3. Spells 4. Weapons 5. Armour 6. Magic item

Magic items	1. Elven cloak
	2. Gauntlets of ogre power
	3. Healing potion
	4. Ring of protection

How to use the table of search encounters

Start from the top and work down. You will enter a building from a door, window or other entrance. There are three possibilities, the entrance will either be open, barred or trapped (DM to decide on this initial set-up). Players can elect to set up traps and barricades on entrances too. Inside a building (or in the street) there may be barrels, crates or chests, the contents of which is decided by rolling a d6 and noting from the table, the corresponding result. If the container is trapped, the players must search for and then disarm the trap; otherwise, they receive -1 HP damage. If the chest contains treasure, roll a d6 to see which treasure from the table is found and roll a further d4 to specify the magic item.

- Creatures include constrictor snake, giant spider, giant rat. DM to choose.
- Hiring NPCs using gold collected from the game can be a useful way for players to strengthen their warband against the monsters in Old Town. Pricing involves spending one gold piece per armour class point of the NPC.
- How much gold is found in a chest is determined by rolling a d20.
- Set barricades on entrances to impede the progress of monsters. A STR [12] is needed to break through. Locked chests need STR [10] to break or unpick the lock with DEX [15].
- Weapons and armour choices – when you find a weapon or armour, roll a d4 to determine the advantage it gives you (maximum +3 with a roll of 3 or 4). See magic items for details of the types of weapons and armour available.
- Spells – healing spells can be used by magical characters to restore HP.
- How to set traps – place a token to represent a trap at an entrance to a building. Any monster who tries to enter that building must first

attempt to search for, and then disarm the trap. See table for ability tests needed.

- How to operate a portal key – when a portal key is found, mark its location with a token. This can then be used to transport to the location of a second portal key. This could come in handy to escape a tricky situation.

Magic items

- Amulet of health – gives you a constitution score of 19.
- Armour (light, medium and heavy) gives you an armour class bonus (+1, +2, +3).
- Elven cloak, by pulling the hood up you gain +1 on wisdom and dexterity checks.
- Gauntlets of ogre power – gives you a strength score of 19.
- Healing potions.
- Spell scrolls.
- Ring of protection – gives you a +1 bonus to armour class.
- Weapon (common, rare, very rare) gives you a bonus to attack and damage (+1, +2, +3).

Monsters

What monsters are involved in the game? Monsters can include an ogre or troll, or group of orcs, goblins or undead raised from the local graveyard. The DM should regulate the difficulty the players face in combatting the monsters. For example, start off easy and ramp up the onslaught of monsters coming to the town as the game progresses, until the players are either destroyed or have the wisdom to retreat to the edge of the board. Monsters will enter from the edge of the board. They move directly towards the players and attack.

Mission to complete.

[DM note] one of the monsters, has (unknowingly) in its possession, the talisman of death. This is a powerful magical item, which the mage would pay dearly for. Do not tell the players about this item. If the players search a defeated monster WIZ [18] they find it "a large pendent with the insignia of a skull" but tell them no more. They can use their own initiative to try and barter it with the mage.

The Dragon's Lair

About the adventure

This is the first encounter that the players have with the dragon. If they have any sense, they won't try to slay him just yet...

[Read aloud] You trek North to the mountainous region where the dragons' den is located. You walk uphill to the mouth of the cave in which the dragon resides. A harsh smell of burning oozes from the entrance and you summon all your courage to go inside. Before you, the dragon rests upon an enormous heap of treasure. He raises his head and turns around to address you. You step back in terror at the same time as reconning whether your fellowship is strong enough to slay the dragon and take the treasure. At this point, the dragon speaks up, saying "why has a hero come to my abode? Does he seek treasure, or want my assistance, or perhaps he wishes to die?"

- Loot the dragon – players can collect treasure tokens (roll d8 to determine how many gold pieces they pick up), while others fend off the dragon's attacks. They can retreat to the edge of the table with the treasure then share it as desired.

- Interact with the dragon – he is boastful and reveals clues to his identity (note that the dragon is in fact the mage, who used a spell from the book to transform into a dragon). However, players must be polite, and a charisma roll of [14] is needed to avoid insulting the dragon. Otherwise, he will attack. [Read aloud]: You cunningly complement the dragon on his appearance, and he decides not to attack you.

- Further interactions – players can question the dragon. What does the dragon know? *(1) the sorcerer was not buried in the tomb; the bones were those of his sacrifices. (2) The treasures were* plundered from Dragon Thorpe and the surrounding towns. (3) The ogre in the woods is under his command. (4) The spell book and shrine in the sorcerer's tomb were written by the mage. Don't reveal that the dragon is the sorcerer. If the players ask any question that fits one of these answers, read them aloud.

- Sorcerers' sword collected from the tomb causes vulnerability to the dragon (doubles hit dice/score).
- Combat the dragon or escape and return to this adventure another day when you are well equipped to destroy a dragon.

This is the final part of the adventure, where the players must face the dragon in a final encounter to rid Old Town of the tyranny that it has caused. The players must seek out the dragon in its lair in the mountains and discover a way to kill this mighty foe.

[Read aloud] As you approach the dragon's mountain lair, you hear a loud rumbling noise. You tentatively peer into the cave entrance towards the dragon's den. There you spot the dragon laid upon its piles of treasure snoring contentedly. What do you want to do?

The Dragon's Den

[DM note] The dragon lives in the large central cavern in this cave system, which also includes three smaller caverns. The players can choose to enter the dragon's lair and explore the cave while it sleeps, making a DEX [14] stealth test while they do so.

- Explore the piles of treasure – [Read aloud] You notice that most of the treasure is in crude nuggets, as it would be straight out of the mine. Among the piles of gold, you find three elaborately decorated chests, inviting you to look inside them.
- Player can look inside the chest labelled 1-3, the contents of which are given in the table below.

Chest 1 – You open the chest, and a beautiful, captivating song erupts from inside. It wakes the dragon, but even still, you find it hard to stop listening to the song. [DM note] the players are bewitched. One must make a CON [12] saving throw to shut the lid of the chest to stop the music and escape the dragon's wrath.

Chest 2 – You open the chest and a green gas escapes out from inside. Make a CON [14] saving throw to avoid d6 damage.

Chest 3 – You open the chest and find it contains six healing potions, resembling those that were brewed at the wizard's apothecary.

- Explore the recesses of the cave – [Read aloud] as you search along the wall, in the dim light of the cave you notice three narrow passages leading into smaller caverns. Do you want to explore these further?

- Attempt to wake the dragon carefully and engage in conversation (return to part 4 of the adventure).

- Make a surprise attack on the dragon. It awakens slightly injured and very annoyed.

Cavern 1

[Read aloud] You squeeze through the narrow passageway into an empty cavern. There is a pool of dark blue water at the far side of this chamber of the cave.

- Investigate the pool – [Read aloud] As you look closer at the pool, you see that it appears to be a flooded mineshaft. It is difficult to fathom how deep the water is.

- Dive into the pool – [Read aloud] The water is cold and deep. You find it hard to hold your breath (CON [12] saving throw) but as you reach the bottom, you discover that the shaft leads around a bend and up another shaft. (Move to cavern 3).

Cavern 2

[Read aloud] Another narrow passage leads into the middle chamber, which is empty except for an abandoned mineshaft in the centre of the cavern.

- Investigate the mineshaft – [Read aloud] the mineshaft is around 30 ft deep and quite narrow.

- Make an intelligence test INT [16] to see what the players know about the mine – [Read aloud] judging from the crude gold nuggets piled in the large centre chamber, surrounding the dragon, this was a gold mine. The narrow diameter of the shaft is too small for a human to climb down. Only a dwarf or halfling would fit. (Note that only player characters that are dwarves/halflings can climb down. Players may need to hire an NPC matching this description). The mine is too deep to jump down, a rope would be needed to lower an adventure down.

Down the mineshaft

[Read aloud] You climb down the rope to the bottom of the mineshaft. You find a network of other tunnels created by the dwarves in their search for gold. Some of the tunnels lead on right underneath the large central chamber, home to the dragon. You contemplate the weight of all that piled gold and large monster hovering above your head. There is nothing else of any significance in the tunnels, the gold has long-since been pickaxed out. Do you want to return to cavern 2?

[DM note] three sticks of explosive can be set in these tunnels underneath the dragon's lair and lit. The players can then attempt to escape the dragon's cave silently and wait for the explosives to go off and kill the dragon inside the cave, as its ceiling falls in on top of the monster.

Cavern 3

[Read aloud] The passageway into this cavern in blocked by fallen rubble left behind from a historic cave-in. You judge that it would take some time to clear a way through. What do you want to do?

- Clear away the rubble – this process takes several turns, depending on the success of a strength ability test taken by the player(s) STR [15-20] the rubble is cleared in 4 turns; STR [10-15] the rubble is cleared in 8 turns; STR [0-10] the rubble is cleared in 12 turns. If another player chooses to help, half the time is taken.

Inside cavern 3

[Read aloud] Inside the cavern, you find a flooded mineshaft and the remains of a long-dead person close by, surrounded by fallen rocks.

- Investigate the body – [Read aloud] the body is that of a dwarf miner. Amongst his accoutrements, you find some potentially useful equipment including: a length of rope, an old cloak (note this is a cloak of deception – see magic items list for details), a pickaxe and three sticks of explosives.

Map of the dragon's den

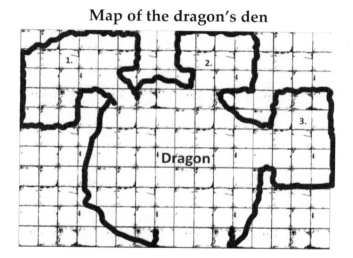

The final encounter.

[Read aloud] after tirelessly questing for months, finally you have killed the dragon and freed Old Town from tyranny. You will go down as heroes throughout history.

D&D

MS

Miniatures used in the artwork available from
EM4 miniatures.

Thank you for playing!

Printed in Great Britain
by Amazon

25242564R10106